THIS BOOK
BELONGS TO

_____

The CARROT, the EGG, and the TEA BAG

A. M. Marcus

Once upon a time there was a smart, talented young girl named Sharon.

4

She worked very hard at being a good student and took part in ballet, spelling bees, and several other activities at school. Like many girls, Sharon was happy...most of the time.

One day, as Sharon walked home from school, she decided to stop and see her father at his restaurant. She was feeling quite overwhelmed and needed someone to talk to.

Sharon thought about her upcoming ballet recital, her math test in two days, and the next spelling bee competition the following week.

When Sharon entered the restaurant, her father noticed her immediately. He paused his work, said hello, and gave her a big hug.

When they sat down, he immediately noticed that she seemed worried, so he asked, "What is troubling you, Sharon?"

"Oh Dad!" Sharon cried. "There's just so much that I have to do, and I feel overwhelmed! My ballet recital is coming up soon, I have a difficult math test in two days, and I need to prepare for the spelling bee next week. I just don't know how to handle it all!"

Her father gently took her hands and said, "Come with me, Sharon, I want to show you something."

"Let's go inside my private kitchen--in which I make my most special dishes." Sharon was very curious about what her father was going to show her.

Inside the kitchen, her dad took three pots and filled them with water. He placed them each on the stove and lit a fire underneath them.

While they waited for the water to boil, her father showed her three bowls, each with something different in them, and said, "Please examine the items in these bowls, and tell me what you see."

First, she held one of the carrots.
"These are quite firm," she said.
Then she picked up an egg, and it
broke in her hands. "These are fragile,
and are soft and gooey inside."

Next she reached for a tea bag. It was full of little dried leaves that rattled when she shook it.

Once the three pots began to boil, Sharon watched her dad place the carrots in one pot, the eggs in the next pot, and the tea bags in the third pot.

While they waited for them to cook, Sharon moaned impatiently, wondering what all of this could mean.

Finally, her father put the carrots, the eggs, and the tea bags back into their bowls and let them cool. "What do you see now?" he asked. "Has anything changed?" Sharon answered, "No, they are still carrots, eggs, and tea bags; nothing has changed." Her father replied, "Please examine them all just a little closer."

"Go ahead and touch the carrots," her father said. She did so and noted that they were now soft.

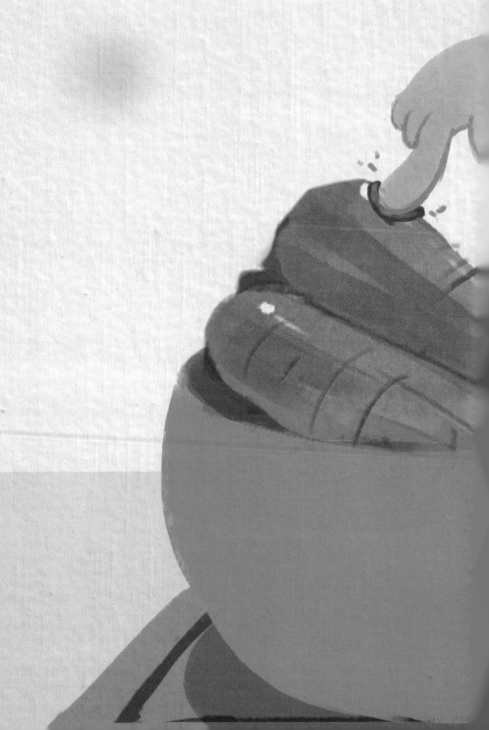

30

He then asked her to take an egg and open it. After pulling off the shell, she observed the hard-boiled egg and stated that it was firm inside, and not soft and gooey like before.

Finally, he removed the tea bags and asked her to taste the water they had soaked in. The rich flavor of the tea brought a smile to her face.

"Father, what does this all mean?" she asked. He then explained that though the carrots, the eggs, and the tea bags had each faced the same challenge--the boiling water--each one had reacted differently.

"The carrots went in firm and solid, but in boiling water became soft and weak."

"Some people are like that. When they face something tough or scary, they become weak."

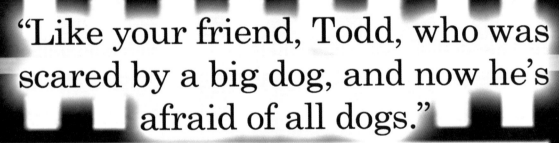

"Like your friend, Todd, who was scared by a big dog, and now he's afraid of all dogs."

"The eggs were fragile, until they were put in the boiling water. Then, the inside of the egg became hard."

"Some people are like the egg. When they go through something difficult, their hearts become hard."

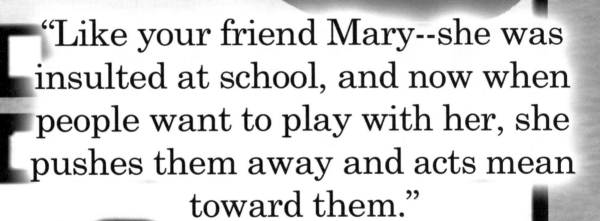

"Like your friend Mary--she was insulted at school, and now when people want to play with her, she pushes them away and acts mean toward them."

"The tea bags, however, are unique. After they were in the boiling water, instead of them changing, rather they changed the water, and created something new--a pot of tea."

"You see, when some people face a challenge, they see it as an opportunity."

"Remember the time we got lost while walking in the city, and we noticed a ballet street performance going on nearby?"

"That's what inspired you to decide you wanted to learn ballet."

"Also take for example, your ballet recital last year, when you mixed up your moves, but ended up creating a new dance."

"This is how something that seems negative can be turned into something positive."

"So, which one are you like?" he asked his daughter. "When challenges come your way, how do you respond?"

"Are you like a carrot,

Sharon thought about how discouraged she had gotten. She didn't like feeling that way. She decided to change her perspective and focus on why she enjoyed each activity and remember why they were important to her.

As she did, she felt less
overwhelmed and more excited!

"My dear child," her father said, "to quote Albert Einstein, who was a very wise man, 'In the middle of difficulty lies opportunity.'"

"You see, Sharon, in life, things happen around us and to us, but the only thing that truly matters is what happens within us, for over this alone, do we have absolute control."

She skipped out the door and headed home. Since she had decided to change the way that she handled her worries, she felt a lot better. She knew now that this was a chance to do her very best. By taking one day at a time, she could use this opportunity to tackle her responsibilities with a positive attitude.

THE END

I remember being your age

I wish that someone had asked me the questions I am about to ask you when I was younger. I know you are very smart and can think for yourself. How would you answer these questions?

- Can you remember a time that you felt overwhelmed, sad, or frustrated?

- Do you remember how you acted? Did you yell and cry, or give up and walk away?

- If you could go back in time, would you react differently?

- Next time you face something difficult, do you think you would like to see it as an opportunity, instead of as a problem?

- Would you prefer to be like the tea bag, instead of the carrot or egg? What does this mean to you?

I would love to know what you think of my book!
Please send me an email: author@AMMarcus.com
or share your thoughts with the rest of the world on Amazon.

Scan and post a review

A word from me to the grown-ups

If your child comes to you angry or frustrated by a challenge or difficulty, help them think critically by discussing the situation with them. By showing children how to think differently, you're helping them hone their creative problem-solving skills, thus allowing them to see opportunities within a challenge or problem.

Research has found that children who display optimism and self-determination in times of difficulty are more likely to overcome the challenges presented to them. It is my hope that this story of The Carrot, the Egg, and the Tea Bag can help your child view themselves as problem-solvers and thinkers.

Have you and your children been inspired?
If you liked this book would you consider posting a review?
Your help in spreading the word is greatly appreciated. Reviews from readers like you make a huge difference in helping new readers find children's books with powerful lessons similar to this book.

I would love to hear from you! Please subscribe to my email newsletter by following the link on the last page.
In the newsletter you will find exciting updates, promotions and more.

Follow this direct link to post a review

go.ammarcus.com/carrot-review

Some personal things about me

My favorite fruits: Strawberries & Raspberries

My favorite school subjects: Math & Computers

My favorite hobby: Dancing & Teaching Salsa

My favorite color: Green

My favorite animal: Tiger

My favorite sport: Soccer

My favorite pet: Dogs

And a little bit more...

I graduated from the Technion Israel Institute of Technology with B.Sc. Cum Laude in Computer Engineering. Throughout my studies, I have been teaching and helping children with math, and through my work, I have helped them to discover their inner strength and motivation to continue studying and nurturing success in life.

I love the challenge of early education, and especially enjoy working with children with learning difficulties. I have found great satisfaction in helping them conquer their fears and overcome the challenges associated with their education.

I have read dozens of self-improvement books, and have been influenced heavily by them. Through self-reflection, I have found that my great dream was to share that wisdom and my numerous life lessons with people, but especially with kids.

I left my computer engineering career in order to pursue my dream of becoming an author of children's books. Today, I continue to write these books, with the goal of teaching kids basic skills through storytelling. I believe that a good story is an excellent way to communicate ideas to children.

Each and every story is based upon some deep issue, value, or virtue that can potentially make a huge impact on the lives of both your children and you. I have a vast collection of quotes, and usually I base my stories off quotes that I personally find inspiring. The lesson of this book, for example, can be summed up in an inspirational quote by Albert Einstein. Turn the page to check the quote.

www.AMMarcus.com

"In the middle of difficulty lies opportunity".

-Albert Einstein

More books
by A. M. Marcus

   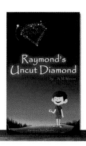 

Coming soon!

Scan to get your FREE GIFT

ammarcus/free-gift

Use the code to get the gift:
277843

Made in the USA
Columbia, SC
22 March 2018